Albertine's Got Talent!

Shena
Power

Illustrated by
Madeline
Valentine

Henry Holt and Company

NEW YORK

Henry Holt and Company, LLC, *Publishers since 1866*
175 Fifth Avenue, New York, New York 10010
www.HenryHoltKids.com

Library of Congress Cataloging-in-Publication Data
Power, Shena.
Albertine's got talent / Shena Power ; illustrated by Madeline Valentine. — 1st ed.
p.   cm.
Summary: Dad is a prize-winning gardener, Mom can speedily sew
complicated outfits, and brother Sam is an expert at soccer, but
Albertine needs help uncovering her hidden talents.
ISBN 978-0-8050-8177-0
[1. Ability—Fiction. 2. Family life—Fiction.] I. Valentine, Madeline, ill. II. Title.
PZ7.P8823Alb 2010   [E]—dc22   2009030625

First edition—2010 / Designed by April Ward
The artist used gouache on hot-press watercolor paper
to create the illustrations for this book.
Printed in May 2010 in China by Macmillan Production (Asia) Ltd.,
Kwun Tong, Kowloon, Hong Kong, on acid-free paper. ∞
Supplier Code: 10

1 3 5 7 9 10 8 6 4 2

To Deborah Feiler,
for your helpful advice,
to Marisa, for taking
Albertine to America, and
as always, to Bruno and Leo
—S. P.

For my mom, my dad,
Turner, and Katie
—M. V.

Albertine's mom and dad and brother, Sam, were the sort of people who were always busy doing things.

Mom had a complicated sewing machine and could run up new outfits for dolls or superheroes in ten minutes flat.

Dad loved growing
vegetables, and his carrots
had won several prizes.

Sam was an expert soccer
player, hoping to be picked by a
professional league talent scout
anytime now.

But Albertine mostly hung around.

"We need to uncover your hidden talents," said Mom.
"We'll get on with it straightaway!"

So the next day after school, Mom took Albertine to Gym Club. "You'll love it!" she said. "They'll teach you back flips, splits, and straddle rolls."

But they didn't.

"Never mind. Gym's obviously not your thing," said Mom.
"Well, what is my thing then?" said Albertine.

The next Monday, Dad took her to a swimming class called Little Flippers. "You'll love it!" he said.

"They'll teach you lifesaving, diving, and floating."

But they mostly taught her
sinking and swallowing water.

"Glug, splut,
ugh, shplut, glug,"

said Albertine.

"Never mind, swimming's obviously
not your thing," said Dad.

On Friday, Mom said, "Right. I've got it. Woodworking!"

Dad said, "You'll love it. They'll teach you sawing, sanding, and planing. You'll probably make a beautiful birdhouse!"

But she didn't. She made a wonky creation that could not even be used as a pencil box.

Mom and Dad said, "Never mind, woodworking's obviously not your thing."

"I agree," said Albertine.

On Sunday morning when they were all having breakfast, Mom said, "Guess what!"

"What?" said Albertine suspiciously.

"Great-Aunt Sophie is coming to tea. Won't that be fun?"

Well . . . Great-Aunt Sophie never smiled,
didn't get jokes, and was usually grouchy at
least once during every visit.

"What shall we do to entertain her?"
asked Mom. "Any ideas?"

"She could help me spread manure
on the vegetables," said Dad.

"She could be goalkeeper,
and I could shoot penalties at
her!" Sam said enthusiastically.

"Maybe she could sew some dolls' clothes with me," said Mom.

"Wait!" shouted Albertine.
"I've got a **brilliant** idea!"

"What's all this?" said Great-Aunt Sophie
that afternoon as she sat down in the special
visitor's chair by the fire.

"Ready? Da dum!

And now a play called *Albertine's Got Talent!*
All the parts will be played by . . .

Albertine acted out all the things that
had gone so horribly wrong.

She acted out the gym class, the swimming lesson, and the woodworking class.

At first Great-Aunt Sophie's face stayed like a stone.
Then it was a stone with creases.
Then it was a stone with cracks.

Then it was a creased, cracked stone with a cave in the middle!
She laughed . . . and laughed . . . and laughed . . . and laughed!

After what seemed like a very long time, she slowly
got to her feet and gave Albertine the most enormous hug.
"BRILLIANT, Albertine!" she said. "You ARE a talented actor!"

"Thank you," said Albertine.
"I think maybe . . .

IT'S MY THING!"